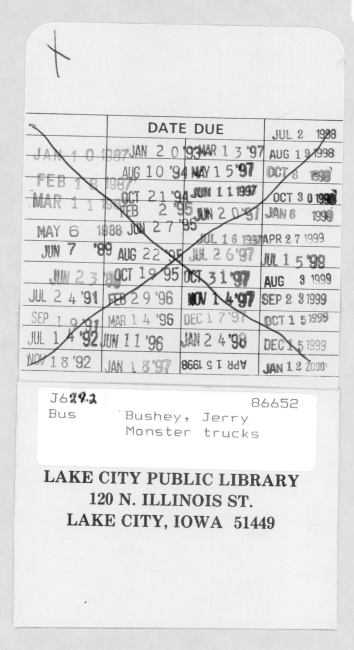

DATE DUE			
			JUL 2 1988
JAN 1 0 1987	JAN 2 0 '93	MAR 1 3 '97	AUG 1 9 1998
FEB 1 8 1987	AUG 10 '94	MAY 1 5 '97	OCT 8 1998
MAR 1 1	OCT 2 1 '94	JUN 1 1 1997	OCT 3 0 1998
	FEB 2 '95	JUN 2 0 '97	JAN 6 1999
MAY 6 1988	JUN 2 7 '95	JUL 1 6 1997	APR 2 7 1999
JUN 7 '89	AUG 22 '95	JUL 2 6 '97	JUL 1 5 '99
JUN 2 3	OCT 1 9 '95	OCT 3 1 '97	AUG 3 1999
JUL 2 4 '91	FEB 2 9 '96	NOV 1 4 '97	SEP 2 3 1999
SEP 1 9 '91	MAR 1 4 '96	DEC 1 7 '97	OCT 1 5 1999
JUL 1 4 '92	JUN 1 1 '96	JAN 2 4 '98	DEC 1 5 1999
NOV 1 8 '92	JAN 1 8 '97	APR 1 5 1998	JAN 1 2 2000

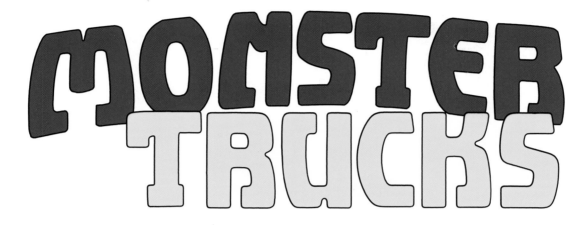

MONSTER TRUCKS

and Other Giant Machines on Wheels

MONSTER TRUCKS

and Other Giant Machines on Wheels

Jerry Bushey

 Carolrhoda Books, Inc./Minneapolis

To Wilfred and Theresa Cheeney, who continue to be an inspiration to me!

The author would like to extend special thanks to the following people and companies for their help in making this book possible: Victor Bromley, American Hoist and Derrick Corporation; Bill Rodgers, Marathon LeTourneau Company; Tom Hayes, Pickands Mather & Company; Peter Mosling, Oshkosh Truck Corporation; Jim Seater and Fred Ridenour, FMC Corporation; and Jo Ann Mattey, National Aeronautics and Space Administration.

The following photographs in this book are reproduced through the courtesy of: back cover (bottom and top left), pp. 5, 9, 10, 11 (both), 12, 13, 14, 15, Oshkosh Truck Corporation; back cover (top right), pp. 3, 16, 17, 18, 19, 20, 21, 22, 24, 25, 26, 27, Marathon LeTourneau Company; pp. 31, 33, 36 (left), FMC Corporation; pp. 34, 36 (right), American Hoist and Derrick Corporation; front cover, pp. 37, 38 (both), 39 (both), 40, National Aeronautics and Space Administration.

Manufactured in the United States of America

LIBRARY OF CONGRESS CATALOGING IN PUBLICATION DATA

Bushey, Jerry.
  Monster trucks and other giant machines on wheels.

  Summary: Text and photographs introduce various large machines with wheels, including a snowblower, a crash truck, a ready-mix truck, and a platform loader.
  1. Trucks — Juvenile literature. 2. Motor vehicles — Juvenile literature. [1. Machinery. 2. Trucks. 3. Motor vehicles] I. Title.
TL147.B86   1985   629.2'24   84-23160
ISBN 0-87614-271-4 (lib. bdg.)

  3   4   5   6   7   8   9   10   93   92   91   90   89   88   87   86

Snowblower

Many of us have seen the little snow-blowers that people sit on or push like lawnmowers to clear their front walks or driveways after a snowfall, but this winter monster isn't called in just to shovel a driveway. One of the world's largest snow-blowers, it weighs about 15½ tons and can blow 50 tons of snow per minute, a weight equal to that of about 50 cars. Its blades, called ribbon blades, stand 6 feet 8 inches tall, and each of its 4 tires is over 4 feet tall. As with most snowplows, the snowblower is a 4-wheel-drive vehicle, which means that the engine powers all 4 wheels for good traction on snow and icy surfaces. A snowblower this huge is used to clear airport runways or to open up roads where snowfalls are heavy. It can operate for 9½ hours on one 200-gallon tank of fuel.

Crash Truck

Another remarkable truck you're likely to find at an airport is the crash/fire/rescue vehicle, also called the crash truck. Crash trucks are built to make time. An 8-wheel truck takes just 35 seconds to reach a speed of 50 miles per hour. A crash truck at the Casper, Wyoming, airport was able to extinguish two flaming jet engines just 47 seconds after firefighters had been notified of a crash landing. Another truck in the Bahamas chased a navy plane down the runway after the pilot had made an emergency landing with one engine in flames. The truck crew was there to put out the fire as soon as the plane had come to a stop.

In addition to being speedy, a crash truck must handle well and have good traction whether on or off the runway. The body of the truck is built in a special way so that the truck can keep all its tires on the ground even when the ground is uneven. In addition, as with the snowblower, a crash

truck's engines (it has two big diesels) power all 8 of its wheels.

Of course, the most important part of a crash truck is its pumping system. An 8-wheel truck can carry a load of fire extinguishing materials consisting of 4,000 gallons of water and 500 gallons of chemical that weigh 40,000 pounds. As they are sprayed from the turrets on the front and on top of the cab, the water and chemical are mixed together to make a foam. Often the top turret is equipped with a special nozzle that can punch through metal so that foam can be sprayed inside a burning plane. The top turret can spray up to 1,600 gallons of foam per minute, and the front turret can spray 300 gallons per minute. Additional foam can be sprayed from two hand-held hoses that attach to the truck's side.

Crash trucks come in different sizes and are to some extent custom built to fit the special needs of the airport firefighting

Diagonally opposite wheels are raised up on 14-inch blocks to demonstrate how a crash truck's special body design works to keep its wheels in contact with the ground for good traction.

units that buy them. For example, a crash truck that will be used in very cold climates will have a heated and insulated storage tank so that its load of water won't freeze even when the temperature drops to -50°F.

Smaller 4-wheel crash trucks cost an average of about $170,000 each, while the larger 8-wheel trucks can cost up to $450,000 apiece, but whatever their costs, sizes, or special equipment, crash trucks make air travel safer for all of us.

Ready-Mix Truck

The ready-mix truck (opposite page) carries up to 28 tons of wet concrete in its mixer—enough to build a wall 3 feet high, 1 foot thick, and 90 feet long. In addition, it packs 3,200 pounds (383.7 gallons) of water in the tank behind the driver's cab.

The ready-mix trucks we usually see unload their concrete through chutes located at the rear. The chute can't be seen from the cab, so extra workers are needed to help the driver back up and guide the chute. All of the trucks shown here, however, have their chutes in front, extending from platforms where workers can add water to the concrete or hose off dirty equipment. By placing the chute in front, the driver can control it and easily move the truck forward while pouring curbs or sidewalks. From within the cab, the driver can automatically lengthen the chute to 12 feet. By adding two extra sections carried on the truck's side, the chute can be lengthened to 20 feet. Forward-chute trucks like these can deliver from 1 to 1½ more cubic yards of concrete per worker hour than conventional trucks, so it takes fewer workers to do the job.

Because its engine powers all 8 wheels, this rugged truck can travel to construction sites in rough terrain or easily climb up the steep earthen ramps leading from deep excavations. It can also travel on highways at high speeds to carry concrete over long distances.

Platform Loader

This unusual truck, called a platform loader, is used mainly to load big cargo planes. The 42-foot-long platform behind the driver can be raised 13 feet while carrying a load of 40,000 pounds. It can tilt forward or backward and to the right or left, enabling workers to move massive cargoes along its 348 rollers and into a waiting plane. The truck can be driven with the platform either raised or lowered.

Dozer

Most of us have seen bulldozers clanking along on their metal tracks as they push dirt into piles on building sites. The world's largest dozer, however, rolls on 8½-foot-tall tires. Weighing in at 193,000 pounds, it makes the common bulldozer look like a midget. (The heaviest bulldozer with tracks weighs 180,000 pounds, 6½ tons lighter than its 4-wheeled cousin.)

The dozer's blade can be changed to push either coal or dirt. Up to 65 cubic yards of coal or 37 cubic yards of heavier dirt and rock can be pushed at one time. That much coal would be enough to fill a very large bedroom. Controls in the cab allow the operator to raise or lower the blade or tilt it forward, backward, or from side to side.

An enormous 16-cylinder, 860-horsepower engine is fed by a 500-gallon fuel tank, but this engine does not move the dozer forward and backward. It powers an electric generator, which in turn powers four large electric motors connected to each of the wheels. Because the diesel engine doesn't directly power the wheels, it can be run at a constant speed, which makes it last longer than engines that are run at changing speeds.

An on-board computer system helps the operator drive and maneuver this gigantic machine. By individually controlling the speed of each wheel, the computer keeps the wheels from spinning and losing traction.

Log Stacker

If you happen to have a small forest's worth of logs you want moved and stacked, the log stacker is the machine for you. The largest weighs in at 200,000 pounds and can lift 140,000 pounds of logs at one time!

Over 15 feet longer than a typical semi truck, its enormous front tires are 9 feet tall.

At the front of the machine are curved tusks (above) and straight forks (below).

These are attached to a lifting mast that is almost as tall as a four-story building. When they are open, the tusks can fit over a stack of logs 16 feet 8 inches high.

As with the dozer, the log stacker's diesel engine generates power for electric motors on each of the four wheels, and an on-board computer system helps the operator control the stacker's movements. Top speed for this workhorse is 12 miles per hour.

Tree Crusher

At a top speed of only 3¼ miles per hour, the tree crusher crashes through a forest on three strange, wide wheels that look more like barrels on their sides than wheels. And where the tree crusher has passed, there's no longer any forest!

Tree crushers are used in many countries where dense forests need to be cleared to make land for growing food. Weighing 35 tons (100-ton models used to be made), the crusher easily pushes over trees, roots and all, with the 10-foot-high bar at its front. Trees 2 feet in diameter are no match for the crusher. After they have been pushed down, the crusher's wheel blades, called grousers, crush the trunks as the machine

rolls forward, leaving no difficult stumps in the ground. Later, workers return to the field to burn up all the debris from the broken trees.

Although the crusher won't win any road races, it can clear up to six acres of forest land per hour. This saves a tremendous amount of time and labor over the old method of cutting down each tree, then digging or pulling out the stumps.

As with the dozer and the log stacker, the tree crusher gets its power from a diesel engine which generates electricity for electric motors on all three wheels.

24

Front-End Loader

Front-end loaders come in all sizes, but when a big job needs to be done at a mine or quarry, this monster gets the call. Its scoop, called a bucket, can lift 66,000 pounds of coal or iron or copper ore and

load it into a truck. The buckets are made of long-lasting steel and can be custom built with different types of teeth and front edges made to order for the kind of material the loader will be scooping.

The powerful 1,200-horsepower diesel engine is fed by a 650-gallon fuel tank and powers electric motors on all four wheels. Although a top speed of 12 miles per hour doesn't sound very fast, that's plenty of speed for a machine that's 53 feet long and weighs 335,000 pounds before it picks up a load.

Each of the loader's four tires is nearly 12 feet tall, costs $45,000, and lasts only 6 months if conditions are *good!* Now you won't be too surprised to learn that the entire machine costs $1,500,000—about 187 times more expensive than the average family car.

One word best describes these spectacular dump trucks: BIG! They are specially designed for continuous use in large mines where millions of tons of ore must be carried from the pits to the processing plants. A mine truck's dump bucket, called the body, can carry up to 170 tons of ore—about the weight of 34 adult elephants.

Some of these trucks are run 24 hours a day until their engines wear out. Miners don't consider this any big deal. It takes them about a day to put in a new engine. Then the truck is restarted and runs until that engine wears out.

As with many of the other machines in this book, the mine truck's diesel engine powers a generator which in turn powers four electric motors that drive the wheels.

Each tire is 10 feet tall and costs $13,000, and these tires last only about 6 months! Every time a new set of tires is needed, it costs $52,000!

Lattice Boom Crawler Crane

If you want to lift something 34 feet, a front-end loader will do the job. If you want to lift something 600 feet, however, you'll need a lattice boom crawler crane. In fact, this crane is powerful enough to easily hoist the loader with a full load in its bucket!

This is the largest type of mobile crane in the world. It weighs 1,000,000 pounds by itself, and the large concrete blocks on its end add another 1,160,000 pounds to help keep it from toppling over when the boom hoists its maximum load of 1,500,000 pounds. Larger models of the same crane in Europe can lift from 2,000,000 to 4,000,000 pounds. Near the top and at the base of the main boom are two smaller booms that help stabilize the crane when lifting such tremendous weights.

This enormous machine is too large to travel over roads unless it is dismantled and carried on several trucks. Just one of the two tracks on which it moves is 35 feet long and requires two semi trucks to transport it from one site to another. The massive concrete counterweight is not transported with the crane. It's cheaper to bury it and then make a new counterweight when the crane is reassembled on a new construction site.

Although the crane can move from spot to spot on a site, before going to work its 70-foot-long body must rest on a concrete pad. The concrete pad acts as a foundation to keep the massive crane from sinking into the ground. The iron rail around the pad's edge guides four sets of wheels, one on each corner of the crane, that support the counterweight and the loaded boom as the crane turns.

Lattice Boom Truck Crane

Lattice boom truck cranes differ from crawler cranes in two major ways—they are smaller and they can be driven on tires instead of metal tracks. This means that they can get to places more easily, and many of them can get there quickly over highways.

The crane pictured on the opposite page has 12 wheels, each of which is powered separately from the others. It can lift up to 165 tons (330,000 pounds). A 100,000-pound counterweight is mounted on the truck's front end. As with the crawler crane, the counterweight helps keep the truck crane from toppling under heavy loads. Truck cranes are further stabilized by "feet" called outriggers, two of which can be seen extending from this crane's near side. This model of truck crane is too heavy to travel on most roads. It is used mainly on waterfronts.

Of the two 8-wheel truck cranes pictured on the following page, the larger model on the left can hoist up to 140 tons of weight. Its boom has a maximum length of 230 feet.

The smaller crane on the right is capable of lifting up to 40 tons. Unlike their 12-wheeled cousin, both of these cranes are light enough to travel over highways.

Crawler Transporter

The driver (above) operates the crawler from whichever of its two cabs is facing forward. You can see one of these cabs (left) just above the crawler's far-left track, under the top deck.

There is probably no larger overland vehicle in the world than the crawler transporter used by NASA to carry a space shuttle and its launching platform to the launch site. This spectacular machine is 114 feet wide by 131 feet long—bigger than a basketball court. It stands 20 feet high and moves on four double-tracked crawlers,

each 10 feet high and 41 feet long. Each shoe, or section, of a crawler track weighs 2,000 pounds.

Even though it is powered by two 2,750-horsepower diesel engines supplying power to 16 electric wheel motors, the transporter is by far the slowest monster of all the vehicles described in this book. Unloaded, it can move at a maximum speed of 2 miles per hour; loaded, it pokes along at just 1 mile per hour. That's not so bad when you consider that it weighs 6,000,000 pounds even before the shuttle and launching

platform, which add another 11,000,000 pounds, are loaded on top.

It takes the transporter five hours to carry its load from the building where it was assembled to the launch pad. It makes the trip on a special roadway called the crawlerway. The crawlerway is 130 feet wide—almost as wide as an 8-lane freeway.

Special devices in the transporter keep the launching platform level while the

transporter creeps over the crawlerway and up the ramp leading to the launch pad. When it reaches the pad, workers jack the launching platform up on its six 22-foot-tall pedestals while the transporter continues to keep it level. Once the shuttle and launching platform are in position, the crawler transporter backs out from underneath the platform and slowly drives away.